T0065541

The Worst Five Months Ever

KATHARINE WEEKS FOLKES

authorHOUSE®

AuthorHouse™
1663 Liberty Drive
Bloomington, IN 47403
www.authorhouse.com
Phone: 1 (800) 839-8640

Published by AuthorHouse   09/23/2016

ISBN: 978-1-5246-4077-4 (sc)
ISBN: 978-1-5246-4076-7 (e)

Library of Congress Control Number: 2016915633

Print information available on the last page.

Any people depicted in stock imagery provided by Thinkstock are models, and such images are being used for illustrative purposes only. Certain stock imagery © Thinkstock.

This book is printed on acid-free paper.

Because of the dynamic nature of the Internet, any web addresses or links contained in this book may have changed since publication and may no longer be valid. The views expressed in this work are solely those of the author and do not necessarily reflect the views of the publisher, and the publisher hereby disclaims any responsibility for them.

- In **"The Worst Five Months Ever,"** Folkes handles the serious topic of bullying in a clever way without preaching to her young readers.

Peggy Caravantes
Author of *Marooned in the Arctic: The True Story of Ada Blackjack: The "Female Robinson Crusoe"; The Many Faces of Josephine Baker: Dancer, Singer, Activist, Spy; prize-winning Daughters of Two Nations.*

- This is a compelling story about bullying but also about forgiveness and compassion. The drama unfolds when Travis, who is being bullied, makes a decision to confront his situation. Will it work? Will his resentment and anger disappear or will his bullies prevail? This is a story of personal growth.

Lupe Ruiz-Flores
Author of *The Woodcutter's Gift*

- Every child who has encountered bullying will relate to fifth grader Travis' dilemma at being bullied in **The Worst Five Months Ever** by Katharine Folkes. This heart-felt story sprinkled with subtle humor and interesting characters, draws us into his anger and resentment at being bullied. After turning the tables and bullying his tormentor, he is faced with guilt and the need to make a difficult decision, thus learning a valuable lesson. **The Worst Five Months** Ever is a must read for all children who have ever seen or been the target of bullying.

Maritha Burmeister,
Author of the prize-winning book, *The 12 Dog Days of Christmas in New York City.*

ACKNOWLEDGEMENTS

Thanks to my smart and beautiful girls—daughter, Katharine and granddaughter, Katya who said, "Go for it!"

Huge amounts of gratitude to my wonderful and talented weekly critique group friends—published authors, all—Peggy Caravantes, Lupe Flores and Maritha Burmeister for their encouragement and valuable input.

Thanks to my sibs, Pat, Miriam and Dick for their "You can do it, sis!" pats on the back.

A thumbs-up to my friends, Meredith, Dana, Molly, Glynda, Judy and Sandra for saying, "It'll happen one of these days!"

I would also like to thank King Kleberg who kindly read my story when he was 10 and gave me his opinion.

CHAPTER ONE

THE TRAYCHES

There should be a law against bullies. I'm serious. They should have to do some kind of community service like cleaning out people's garages or attics, or heck, clean the room of the kid they bullied. Yeah! That's it.

My twin cousins, Howie and Homer Hall are the worst bullies ever and they live next door! Howie's the meanest but Homer's no angel. I call them the "Trayches," for the triple H-es, but not where they can hear me. They're like some creepy contagious disease that keeps attacking me. I've talked to Grandpa about it and also to my friend, Tim Duncan of the San Antonio Spurs. Well, actually I talk to him in my head. He's my hero and he'd probably say, "Stay cool, Travis and watch your mouth." I try to, honest, but sometimes I just can't.

Take this afternoon—I was out in our driveway shooting baskets while I waited for supper when I heard...

"Hey, Roach Face! You're trespassing!"

Naturally I don't like the name, Roach Face, but it's just Howie's typical grossness—it doesn't have anything to do with the way I look, so it doesn't bother me all that much. If he called me Carrot-top or Freckles or Shorty, I'd hate it big time, but he hasn't figured that out yet and I guess Roach Face was the worst thing he could think of.

My ball had bounced off the rim of the net over into the Trayches' yard. I was halfway there, but Howie was closer. He clomped down his front porch steps, moving fast for his size, Homer right behind him. They must have radar or something. Or they were spying on me.

I glared at Howie. "I'm just getting my basketball."

He leaned down "You want it? One dollar."

I stood my ground like Dad told me to. "I don't have to give you a dollar, and I wouldn't if I had one!" I reached for my ball. Howie grabbed it and tossed it to Homer.

Okay, different strategy: "You want to shoot some baskets?"

Howie sneered. "Nice try, dork. Ball's ours now."

I tried a quick grab but Howie shoved me and I tripped. Getting up, I glanced at Homer.

He looked away.

One more try. "Come on, guys. Give my ball back, please."

Howie sneered, like me saying please was pitiful and wimpy. "Please? Let's see. I don't think so." Howie said, grinning and punching Homer on the arm. Then they went back in their house. With my basketball!

I was so mad I kicked acorns like I was kicking field goals across our connecting yards back to my house. Inside, I tried to get past the kitchen without Mom hearing me. She was tired of my complaints about the twins and I was tired of even thinking about them. Mom's a child psychologist and I truly believe she'd diagnose my cousins as socially challenged if she weren't their mom's sister. And here's the bummer of all bummers. Not only do they live next door, they're in my fifth grade class. I can't get away from them. Ever.

"Travis? You're sneaking. What happened?"

Mom truly does have eyes in the back of her head. And super-sensitive ears. One time she actually heard me chewing a caramel. Seriously.

"Nothing. I was just trying to get my basketball back. Howie stole it."

"Just stay away from him and let things cool down."

"Okay, but I want my basketball back!"

I went to my room and started on my homework, but I must have read the same sentence three times. I kept thinking about Homer, who is a total mystery to me. For some reason he acts like he's programmed to copy everything Howie does. I know they're twins and all, but they're not identical. If Howie laughs at somebody, so does Homer. If Howie calls somebody something bad, Homer does, too. Or at least, he agrees with it. Thing is, Homer's a lot smarter than Howie, so why can't he just be himself? Probably because Howie's so mean he'd beat up his own brother if he didn't do what he said.

Another thing. They don't even try comebacks. The other day when I asked Howie if he knew he had one ear lower than the other, he punched me! I wasn't being mean, I was just curious. If somebody had told me *I* had one ear lower than the other, I'd have probably said something like "'Course it is. It's for listening to kids shorter than me." Easy.

But listen to what happened today. In Mrs. Parks' fifth grade class, we're studying past presidents. At school this morning I was ready to give my report on Teddy Roosevelt. I had a couple of props: a fake mustache and these glasses called a pince-nez that Grandpa loaned me that used to belong to *his* grandpa. Mr. Roosevelt wore some just like them. They don't have any side pieces, just this curved part that goes over your nose. I don't know how he kept them on when he rode a horse—all that bouncing.

Anyway, the glasses were on my desk ready to put on when it was my turn. Howie and Homer came in just as the buzzer sounded and bumped down the aisle, banging the desks on both sides with their big selves. Howie bumped extra hard into my desk and knocked the glasses on the floor. He looked down and back up at me and then he stepped on them! "Oops," he said.

I picked them up. One lens looked like a car's windshield that'd been in a crash and the middle part was all bent. Grandpa was going to kill me. No, he was going to be sad, and that was worse.

In the car, after school, I showed them to Mom. She was super mad. Before I could say anything she said, "Travis, your grandpa trusted you with those. They're a special keepsake."

"Mom, wait a minute. Howie bumped into my desk and knocked them on the floor. When I reached for them, he stepped on them. On purpose! Then he laughed and said, "Oops."

Her expression changed. "Oh. I'm sorry. I shouldn't have jumped on you."

We took them straight to an optometrist who said he could fix them, thank goodness. When we got home I was going to go to Grandpa's to tell him what happened, but I started thinking about Howie and I got mad all over again. He owed me an apology, and he owed Grandpa one, too. And he still had my basketball. I went over to his house. Aunt Karen opened the door.

"Hi, Travis."

"Hi, Aunt Karen. Um, could Howie come out for a minute?"

She looked at me. I could see her trying to figure out if me being there was good or bad, but she said, "Come in and I'll get him."

I shook my head. "Thanks, I'll just wait out here."

I was looking at their pumpkins when Howie opened the door. "Yeah?"

I looked him straight in the eye. "You didn't say you were sorry about Grandpa's glasses. And I want my basketball back." He started to close the door in my face but I grabbed the edge of it to keep it open. Then he slammed it! On my fingers! I yelled. He opened it just enough for me to yank my hand out, then slammed it again. "Ow! Ow! Oooooooo…Geeeeez!" It hurt something fierce. Stupid, stupid, stupid! I didn't get my basketball and I probably had four broken fingers. When I got home, Mom made me wrap them in a dish towel with ice in it. Just about froze my hand off and my fingers swelled up anyway.

After supper I rode my bike over to Grandpa's to tell him about his glasses. He only lives four blocks away, all by himself since Gran died last year. It's a house called a garden home, which is a good name for it because Gran had a vegetable garden out back. Grandpa still keeps it up and grows all kinds of stuff.

On the way over, I thought of how I'd punish Howie if it was up to me. First, I'd lock him in his room with no food. That'd get him! Plus he'd get "F's" for not showing up at school. Then, after I let him out, I'd give him squash and okra. Ha!

I hated to tell Grandpa what happened, but at least he'd be open minded. He'd listen to the whole thing first, *then* give advice. He's a real advice-machine. I have to say, usually it's pretty good, though most times it's too late to help me any. I speeded up and tried to pop a wheelie, but it hurt my hand. I skidded into his driveway and dropped my bike.

Grandpa came to the door, his white hair hanging down in his face, as usual. He looked me over and shook his head. "Well, aren't you a Gloomy Gus."

I gutted up. "Grandpa, I've got to tell you something, and, um, you're not gonna like it."

He squinted at me. "Spit it out, son, whatever it is, and let's take a gander at it."

I told him and held my breath.

He walked back inside. I followed. Sitting in his chair, he motioned me to the ottoman. He took his time answering. "Travis, what happened wasn't your fault. And from what you say, I don't think there was any way you could've prevented it. Howie does things sometimes I just don't understand. I'll tell you somethin' though, maybe you ought to think about." He took off his own glasses and started cleaning them with his shirt tail. "Sometimes people act bad because something's goin' on in their lives that's got 'em upset and they lash out from frustration. Know what I'm sayin'?"

I knew what he was saying all right, but Howie's been lashing out his whole life. He's been a bully forever. I think he was born one.

Grandpa continued, "I'm sorry about the glasses, but you've worried enough. And you got 'em fixed, that's good. Anyway, worrying never accomplished anything. So...what's next on the agenda? Why are you holding your hand like that?"

I told him what happened and he went in the kitchen and got a dishtowel and some ice. "We'll just wrap it up and let the swelling go down and then we'll take another look at it."

"But Mom already put ice on it. And I can wiggle my fingers. See?"

He wrapped it up, anyway. "What'd you expect, boy? Stick your hand where it doesn't belong, you're askin' for trouble."

The ice was really cold. "Grandpa, I'm gonna get frost bite!"

"No you're not. Give it a while longer."

While we waited, we talked about Howie. "That boy seems to have a chip on his shoulder big as a house," Grandpa said. "I've tried talkin' to him, but he doesn't listen and it's not my place to discipline him. Up to his parents."

I told him about the time I asked Howie about his uneven ears and he'd punched me just for asking a simple question. "I was just curious about 'em, Grandpa. He didn't have to hit me."

Grandpa sighed. "Well, now, that's a different story. Come here, son. Look at me up close. See my left eye? Smaller than my right, ever notice that?"

"No, sir, but now that you mention it..."

"Used to be self-conscious about it. Punched a kid dumb enough to bring it to my attention."

I stared at him. "You're saying it's okay to punch somebody?"

"Naw. That's not what I'm saying. I'm saying don't go being nosey about a person's appearance. Leave 'em be about it. In other words, mind your own business."

I took the ice off my fingers. I couldn't stand it any longer. They were so cold I could hardly feel them, and I was still mad. "Okay, but I wish I *had* punched Howie, 'cept I probably would've hit the dang door instead of his face, he closed it so fast."

Grandpa chuckled. "Never aim at something you're not sure is there, son. I learned that one time I was aiming at a dove. Turned out I shot a killdeer—which by the way, is a bird. Poor little fella, not even worth eatin'." He reached over and felt all over my fingers. "I don't think they're broken." Then he grinned. "But if they turn black, you'll know I was wrong." He got up. "Come on out back and help me pick some squash. You can use your left hand. Take some to your mother. You like squash?"

"Um, not really."

"You should. Like all vegetables. They're good for you."

"Yes, sir, I know."

I have to say, this time Grandpa's advice was on overload. I rode home with a grocery sack full of squash and tomatoes and okra hung over my handlebar. It was so full my knee hit it every time I pedaled. I hoped I wasn't banging up the tomatoes. I didn't care about the squash and okra, I wouldn't have to eat those. Mom and I'd already been down that road.

CHAPTER TWO

MIRACLES DO HAPPEN

Monday was the first day of December, and it was T-shirt weather, but Mrs. Parks had a little red poinsettia plant on her desk to remind us of the season. In San Antonio, Texas, where I live, it can be cold or hot in December. Or both. Everybody keeps their summer clothes where they can get to 'em easy. And hardly anybody wears wool, unless they're old or super cold natured.

Third period we took turns reading *Wonder,* by R.J. Palacio. We were supposed to be "reading with expression." When it was Howie's turn he skipped over a bunch of words and mispronounced the rest (exaggeration, but close). Mrs. Parks finally stopped him. It was pretty embarrassing. "Thank you, Howie. Travis, why don't you read next?" Howie's uneven ears turned red and he flopped back in his seat, glaring at me with a look that meant I was gonna get it.

After school, I was walking out to the driveway, and all of a sudden my knees were knocked out from under me from behind. "Think you're so smart, don'tcha, Mr. Show-off reader?" Howie hissed.

I got up. That was it. I'd had it! It was the third time he'd attacked me in a week. It wasn't my fault if he had dyslexia or something, and I hadn't asked Mrs. Parks if I could read.

I exploded. "Old lop-sided tomato ears can't read because his brain is probably lop-sided, too," I yelled. I didn't care who heard me. I grabbed my backpack and headed for the car-rider line to wait for Mom.

I hadn't gone hardly any distance when I was grabbed and yanked around. Howie's face was the same color as his ears. I didn't wait to get hit. I head butted him smack in the stomach. Then I ran. He's bigger than me. Did I mention that?

I saw Mom, five cars back in line, and I ran and jumped in. I told her what happened. Well not *exactly* what happened. I think she figured I'd left something out, because instead of sympathy, I got, "Oh, Travis, not again."

So I sat there, staring out the window, feeling sorry for myself. I hate Howie Hall, cousin or no cousin, and I'm not one bit sorry about what I called him. He's the meanest person I've ever known! When we were finally out of the school driveway Mom turned off on this side street out of traffic and stopped.

Uh-oh. Here it comes.

But she took my hand and gave me one of those good "mom-looks" I don't get a whole lot of. "Travis, of course I'm sorry he did that to you," she said. "He shouldn't have. And I'll speak to Aunt Karen about it. Not that it does much good," she added kind of under her breath. "But listen to me a minute. This... whatever it is between you and your cousins has been going on way too long and it has got to stop. I know Howie gets out of line, but maybe you antagonize him. Sometimes I have the feeling you don't tell me everything." She gave me a meaningful look. "However, you're a smart boy. Figure out a way to prevent these incidents. Use your head."

That was semi-funny. I *had* used my head, and it hurt my neck, to tell you the truth. But I hadn't *exactly* told her that part, either. "Mom, I don't start these things. They do. Mostly Howie does. What am I supposed to do? They're mean, and I'm tired of getting beat up and picked on! I wish they weren't my cousins! I wish we could un-relate ourselves."

She smiled and squeezed my hand. "How many times have you heard that problems are never solved by running away?"

I tried for humor. "Yeah, but problems aren't the ones getting beat up."

Humor bombed, and she wasn't finished. "Now, I want you to put that good brain to work and figure out a solution. They're going to be your cousins for the rest of your life, so you'd better learn to make the best of it."

"It's not fair!" I fussed.

She gave a short laugh. "We don't get to choose our relatives, darlin', but you *can* choose to get along with them."

"Yes, ma'am." That was it. Lecture over. Grownups sure do like to lecture. Maybe they save up all the advice that was preached to them when they were kids and when they're adults they finally let it all out.

When I got home, I went to my room and forgot about the twins. I pulled the sign-up sheet for the school Holiday Sing-along out of my backpack. There'll be Christmas carols and songs for Hanukkah and Kwanzaa, and we can invite our parents and grandparents and friends to come. I definitely want to do it. I love Christmas.

Next day at school, I turned in the sign-up sheet and walked back to my desk. Howie and Homer came in, bumping down the aisle as usual, but their faces looked different. Kind of closed up. They didn't say anything to anybody or look at anybody. Weird.

During lunch period, when I went to the restroom, I heard this noise like somebody was trying to stop bawling. It was coming from one of the stalls. Whoever it was must've heard me come in, because he started coughing to cover it up. After a minute he came out, swiping his eyes with his sleeve. He grabbed a paper towel and held it up to his face. Then he saw me. It was Howie!

"Travis, if you tell… "

I just stared at him. "I won't. You okay?" Dumb question.

He banged his fist on the wall. He was definitely not okay. I moved out of punching range, but I had to say something. "What happened?"

His breath kind of exploded out and his voice was all shaky. "Mom and Dad are getting a divorce! And we've got to change schools in the middle of the year. During Christmas vacation! Did they pick a good time, or what?"

Wow. That was news to me. "Why can't you keep going to school here?"

His face was all splotchy and he was sucking in air so fast it made his head jerk. He closed his eyes and tried to stop. "Mom couldn't find a house in this school district. (suck, suck) At least not with rent (suck) she could afford."

Howie kind of folded over, holding his stomach like somebody'd hit him. Then he blurted, "And to top it off, Dad's leaving town! He's deserting us!"

"Uncle Henry? Where's he going?"

Howie snorted, "Away from us."

This was sure a different Howie from the usual horrible one. But all I could think of was how mean he'd always been to me. Why should I care about him even if he was my cousin? That fact sure never got in *his* way. I stood there feeling mixed up.

All of a sudden I remembered what Grandpa said about people acting bad because of something going on in their lives. Had he known about Aunt Karen and Uncle Henry getting a divorce? Howie was sure right about one thing. They couldn't have picked a worse time. 'Course I don't guess there's ever a good time.

I actually felt sorry for him. "I'm really sorry, Howie."

I watched "sad" leave his face and that old mean look take its place. "I don't need your sympathy, roach-face. The only good thing about this is I'll be moving away from you!" His nose was running, big time. He reached up, grabbed another paper towel and left.

I stood there a minute. Whatever sympathy I'd felt for him was gone. And I mean totally! And miracle of miracles—he'd be out of my life! I looked up toward heaven.

Thank you!

CHAPTER THREE

"IT IS A WISE FATHER THAT KNOWS HIS OWN CHILD"

—from Shakespeare's *Merchant of Venice*
(one of my Dad's quotes when he thinks I'm holding something back or he
wants to "compliment" me into doing something)

That night at the supper table, Mom and Dad looked at me sort of funny. I couldn't tell what was coming. Funny looks can go either way.

Dad cleared his throat. "Travis, your mother and I have made a big decision..." he cleared his throat again—not a good sign—"and its success will depend for the most part on you."

My mind raced. Were they adopting another kid? Or worse, were they *getting a divorce, too?* I almost panicked. Mom smiled. Sort of.

"As you can imagine," Dad continued, "your Aunt Karen is very upset right now, and we want to help her. We think the breakup of their family will be less traumatic for them if the boys don't have to transfer to a new school in the middle of the year. Sooo, we have decided to let them stay here with us until school's out, except for weekends which they will spend with her."

I felt like the mother of all Tsunamis had hit me. I almost threw up. This was worse than being grounded for a year. I stared at him. "You're kidding, right?"

He shook his head.

"Dad, they hate my guts! It's bad enough they live next door, but in my house? They'll poison me in my sleep! I'll be dead in a week!"

Dad put his hand on my arm. "We know it won't be easy, son. We're aware of their antagonistic ways and Howie's mean-spiritedness." He paused. There was probably a 'however' coming. He continued. "We are also aware, however, (yep, there it was.) that you haven't exactly been an innocent, yourself." He stopped a minute for that little fact to sink in.

Doom and gloom! I'd been so happy when I thought they were moving, and now this. Talk about your highs and lows!

Mom spoke up. "Travis, I know you've had a tough time with the twins, but now's your chance to prove your mettle."

"Metal? What metal?"

She took my hand. "Prove what you're made of. I know you can get along with them if you put your mind to it. And since they'll be in this house, we'll keep an eye on them."

I looked down at my unfinished supper. So much for being hungry.

Mom squeezed my hand. "Now, I want you to promise you'll do your best to help us get through this difficult time. Can we depend on you?"

She looked so hopeful. I glanced at Dad. "This has to be a family effort," he said. "All for one and one for all!" Dad teaches English Lit., college level, and is always quoting famous writers. Sometimes when they're not even English. He raised his hand for a fist-bump.

I bumped. What choice did I have? "I'll try, Dad, but it won't be easy."

"That's my boy! I knew we could count on you. Bravo!"

Sheesh! I felt like a yo-yo. Up, down, up, down. But I grinned and he patted me on the shoulder.

There's nothing like praise. Even if it's for something you've agreed to that you don't see any way you can do. It made me think of a song on one of Gran's CDs she used to play. This guy tells the girl he'll give her the moon. I always thought that was funny. He knows there's no way he can do it, but the girl thinks he's awesome for saying it. That's how I felt about my promise to try to get along with the Trayches.

"Your heart is in the right place, Travis," Mom said.

Well, boy, my mouth sure wasn't. Suddenly I realized how long it would be that they'd live with us. I looked at Mom, and gulped. "Mom? That'll be... *five* months!"

"And son," Dad added, "I expect you to make them feel welcome."

~ ~ ~

Talk about mission impossible. That weekend was awful. I spent it moving *my* stuff and my clothes into the guest room. I couldn't believe it. Because it had a queen sized bed, Mom said it wouldn't work with the two boys, so they got my room and my twin beds. *And* my favorite posters, except my Tim Duncan poster. I took that one with me. And they got my desk. I would have to do my homework on a rickety old card table. Great. So much for "doing the right thing." What'd it get me? Kicked out of my own room. And I'd have to share my bathroom with them. For five months!

Their house next door sold the first week it was on the market. Howie and Homer would be out of my life (at least for now) if my parents hadn't agreed to keep them. I felt like they'd signed my death warrant.

CHAPTER FOUR

CATTLE LESSON

The afternoon before the twins came, Mom dropped me off at Grandpa's while she ran some errands. I love Grandpa's house. He's got this big leather sofa that's old and soft, and these two humongous arm chairs I can stretch across sideways in and read. They used to be at his ranch down near Laredo. There's two guest rooms, one for me and one for Howie and Homer, but I don't think they hardly ever come. In my room there's this picture of Blue Boy, Grandpa's Australian cattle dog. He was a Blue Heeler, but he died a long time ago. Grandpa doesn't have a dog now. I wish he did. I wish I did! I keep asking for a puppy. Maybe I'll get one for Christmas. That would be the best present ever!

Grandpa was working on a puzzle he'd set up on a card table in the den.

"Pull up the ottoman and help me out, here," he said.

I knelt on the ottoman and looked at the picture on the box. It was all these different kinds of cattle. I told him about what was going on at my house, while he told me about the cattle. It was a weird conversation.

"Grandpa, *you* know how mean Howie and Homer are. I don't want them living with me!"

"I don't blame you one bit, son. Now, see that one right there? That's what you call a Santa Gertrudis. They were bred to resist the Texas heat and insects, which as you know, we have plenty of."

I found a puzzle piece and put it in. "Yes, sir. It looks like the one in the picture over the fireplace. But Grandpa, I had to move out of my own room!"

"Now that doesn't seem right, does it?" He looked up at me and then back at the puzzle.

"But you're right about the picture. Same breed, but this un's a cow. Now lookee there. That's an angus, and over there's a longhorn."

"Yes, sir, I know about longhorns. That's like the University of Texas mascot, 'Bevo'."

He chuckled. "Righto, kiddo. Bevo. Now, see if you can find the piece that goes right there."

This mixed up kind of talking went on until Mom came to get me. I didn't exactly get over being mad about the Trayches moving in, but Grandpa and I almost finished the puzzle, and I learned stuff about cattle I never knew before.

When I walked out the door he patted my shoulder. "Travis, be like the Santa Gertrudis. Adjust to the heat."

I guess that meant the "Horrible Halls." That might've been good advice, but it sure wasn't what I wanted to hear!

The next day Howie and Homer moved in. I could tell they'd had "the lecture." They shook my parents' hands and thanked them for their hospitality. That effort must have stretched their manners to the limit because they just walked past me. Here we go, I thought.

Mom had taped a paper welcome sign on the door to their (my!) room. She took Howie and Homer in and showed them where they could keep their things. She'd even put a little decorated Christmas tree up on the chest of drawers. I stood in the doorway and watched them take over my private space, like they had squatters' rights.

Christmas music was coming from the family room. Mom thought it would be festive and lift their spirits. The song was "Deck the Halls."

I wish I could.

CHAPTER FIVE

HOUSE PUESTS

"Hurry up. I gotta pee!" I yelled, banging on the door. The Trayches were hogging the bathroom, as usual. They always raced to get there first in the morning, and then stayed forever.

Mom called us for breakfast. I could smell bacon. The bathroom door slammed open and they raced out, laughing and punching each other. They ran past me to the kitchen. Howie looked back and said, "Hope you don't like bacon. Won't be any left."

They probably *would* eat it all, unless Mom saved me some. At least they liked bacon. They'd been so picky, mealtime at our house was getting to be a problem. I don't know how Aunt Karen stood it. There's not a single vegetable Homer likes except corn on the cob, which Mom said is really a starch, and Howie won't eat any fruit except strawberries. I can tell she's frustrated from all the things they don't like. Sometimes I whistle between bites, or go yum-m-m, but she made me stop.

On our last day of school before Christmas vacation, we had the Sing-along in the auditorium. Fortunately, I didn't have to stand next to the Trayches because they can't carry a tune in a bucket, as Grandpa would say. Why were they in it then, you might ask? Special treatment, that's why. They wanted to be in it, and I think the teacher felt sorry for them. I felt sorry for them, too, but I was really tired of all this special treatment stuff. Especially at my house.

Aunt Karen was sitting next to Mom in the front row. She had a tissue up to her face, and I saw Mom pat her hand. Grandpa was there, too. Dad came in late, but he made it.

We sang "Jingle Bells" and "It's Beginning to Look a Lot Like Christmas." Then we sang the Hanukkah song, Left to Right," about the way to pass the Hanukkah candle. It was a neat song. Next was "Silent Night," and Mom smiled at me and blew me a kiss. I felt my face burn, but I didn't really mind. There were some other songs, then we sang "Seven Days of Kwanzaa." Salim beat the drum with his fingers, and Mom tapped on her purse. We ended the program with "Carol of the Bells," and we played our hand bells. I was beginning to get some Christmas spirit.

That almost came to an end when we went to pick out a tree. Dad took the twins and me to Sonic for milkshakes first, and then we wandered around the tree lot trying to decide on the best one. Naturally, we couldn't agree. Howie started blowing chocolate milkshake through his straw at me. Just as I was ready to blow back, Dad called a halt.

"Okay, guys," he said, "decision time." He looked at the three of us. I strongly felt that since it was my house, and they were guests, ("puests!") I should get to pick. I thought Dad could say, "Boys, let's let Travis choose this time. You've had your way about a lot of things." But no-o-o. They both pointed to the same tree and looked up at him. I was beginning to feel like the outsider, here, and I didn't like it.

Mom could tell, I guess, since I wasn't my normal wonderful self when we got home. After we finished decorating the tree, she let me put the angel on top. Big whopping deal.

Howie and Homer spent the weekend with their mom, but they came back for Christmas break because she had to work. My mom had some vacation time.

The first day was cold and rainy, wouldn't you know it? I got out my Monopoly game and the twins and I sat on the rug in front of the fire and played for hours. We bought houses and hotels, and we were actually having fun. Then Howie landed on some of my property and he had to mortgage some of his. He didn't like that, so he quit.

"Me, too," Homer said.

I got my book, *The Wednesday Wars*, and flopped in a chair to read. The Trayches didn't want to read and got out their phones, but Mom brought in my old two-sided easel and some colored felt pens. She set the easel up by the big window and clothes-pinned some paper to each side. "Express yourselves—anything you like," she said. "If you do a good job, we'll get them framed. Okay?" She smiled and left them to it.

I was sitting near Howie's side. Every now and then I'd glance up to see what he was doing. It took him a long time to decide what to draw, but finally he drew a house. He added the front porch and the big tree in the side yard. I guess it was supposed to be their ex- house next door. He started drawing a Christmas wreath on the door, but he stopped and scribbled all over it. Then he blacked out all the windows in the house. Then he just scribbled all over the whole picture and lay down on his stomach in front of the fire.

I went to get some milk and got a look at Homer's. He was drawing our Christmas tree and the fireplace. It was pretty good, actually.

After a while Mom came in with three long forks and a bag of marshmallows. Homer sat down by Howie and put one on his fork. I joined them and put one on mine. Howie just lay there, staring at the fire.

I stared at it too, thinking I was glad I was me and not them.

CHAPTER SIX

I'M TRYING, TIM

Four days 'til Christmas. It was the Sunday before, and Aunt Karen brought Howie and Homer back from their weekend together. They grumbled and wouldn't look at me. I guess I didn't blame them. I wouldn't want to be living at their house. If they still had a house. After their mom left, they pushed past me and went to "their" room, and closed the door. Great.

I went to my "exile room" and got my basketball. Aunt Karen had brought it back. I looked up on the wall at Tim Duncan—my basketball hero—and wondered what he'd do if he were me. My Christmas spirit was gone, and I was mad at the Trayches. I didn't want them living with me. Not a good way to feel about your own cousins—especially at Christmas. Old Tim would probably tell me to try putting myself in their shoes, and understand how they felt. So would Grandpa. I don't know… maybe.

I knocked on their door. "Guys?"

"Buzz off!" Howie yelled.

"Want to shoot some baskets?"

Nothing. I turned to leave when the door opened.

"It's better than sitting in your stupid old room," Homer said, yanking the ball away from me. I tried to get it back, but he took off down the hall. Racing outside, Homer slammed the ball against the garage door and I caught it. I was swinging around to shoot, when Howie grabbed it from me. We pushed and fouled and grabbed and shot, and never said a word to each other.

After a while Mom came out with her camera. "Okay, boys," she said. "I want to see some crazy shots and crazy faces. The crazier the better."

We looked at her like *she* was crazy. Then Homer laughed. He jumped in the air and hollered, "kawabunga!" and threw the ball. I caught it on the bounce, looked at Mom with crossed eyes, and threw it backwards over my head. Howie grabbed it, danced little bitty steps sideways up to the net, turned and sank the shot. After a few minutes we forgot the crazy stuff, and everybody played for real. Mom clicked away like a professional photographer.

The next day she took us with her to pick up the pictures. We were looking at them and making comments, when Howie said, "I bet Dad doesn't even have any pictures of us. He'll probably forget what we look like."

"You could give him one for Christmas," I said. "Your mom, too."

Score points for me! They seemed to go for that idea. They had some spending money and found two big black picture frames that had a bunch of different sized cut out places for photos. When we got back home they arranged the pictures in the frames and wrapped them for their parents.

On Christmas Eve when they left with Aunt Karen, they actually smiled. Mom gave them each a hug.

"Merry Chris-moose," I called, as they ran down the walk.

Grandpa was standing behind me with his hands on my shoulders. He squeezed and hollered, "Hurry back!"

I stepped on his toe. He chuckled.

I could hardly wait for some time to myself and with my family. Just us. Of course, it was only for one day. But it was a great day!

I had asked for a puppy for Christmas, but Mom told me she didn't think she had the strength to take on that responsibility right now with the twins here. 'Course I'd told her I'd train him and clean up after him, but she just smiled and patted me on the head. Stupid cousins. They ruined everything. But…listen to this! On Christmas morning something wet on my face woke me up. I opened my eyes and there was a full grown yellow lab staring at me! He had a red bandana around his neck. I held his head with both hands, and he licked me again.

Mom and Dad were standing in the doorway, grinning. "Merry Christmas!" Mom said.

I jumped up and gave them both a hug. "This is the greatest Christmas present ever!

What's his name?"

Mom laughed. "*Her* name is Joy. She's one year old this month."

Seems the receptionist at Mom's clinic was moving and couldn't take her dog, so I got to be the lucky new owner!

Grandpa came over for breakfast. He had on a green sweater and a Santa Claus hat, and he walked in the door, squeaking a toy for Joy. He sure was good at keeping a secret. He handed me a Christmas bag with tissue paper sticking out the top. I grinned. It looked so fancy, either the store wrapped it or Mom did. Under the paper was a new Spurs jersey which I needed because my old one shrunk. Or I'd grown.

Joy was already house broken and knew how to sit and stay, no training required. Now I ask you, is that the perfect dog, or what?

When Howie and Homer came back after Christmas they had a ton of presents. It looked like their mom and dad had been in competition with each other to see who could give them the most. It was truly awesome.

"Look at all the stuff we got," Howie bragged.

"Yeah, we made a haul," Homer said, unplugging himself from his new i-Pod.

I looked at all their loot. They'd sure gotten a lot. But I had Joy, and I could tell they were envious.

Most of the time the Trayches stayed in their room with their head phones on, so I didn't have to talk to them much. Between them listening to music and spending the following weekend with their mom, it was pretty quiet around our house. Joy slept in the bed with me and was better company, anyway.

When school started back, Mom made sure we all did our homework in the afternoons, and after that it was time for supper, and for some reason the next two weeks went by pretty fast.

Then Homer came down with something that turned out to be a virus. Howie and I didn't get it at first, but after two days we did. Mom was in and out of our rooms, taking temperatures bringing us water and anything we felt like eating, which wasn't much. She couldn't go to the clinic at all. And the worst part was Aunt Karen was sick, too, and couldn't come get the twins and take care of them for the weekend.

Then Dad got it. Mom said he was more trouble than the three of us put together. Thank heavens for Campbell's Chicken and Stars. That was about all we could eat. And thank heavens Mom didn't get the virus, though I sure don't know why she didn't. God must have known she couldn't—she not only took care of everybody, she had to walk Joy (my job).

When we finally got back to school, half the class was out, including Mrs. Parks. The virus was knocking kids down like bowling pins. But we had a neat substitute named Mr. Flores. He brought a parrot in a cage that actually got to stay in our class. The parrot's name was Jorge, (pronounced Hor-hay) which is Spanish for George, and he was bilingual. Can you believe it? And get this—Mr. Flores let the parrot help teach us Spanish. How cool was that?

"You kids could go on TV as the only kids who speak Spanish with a parrot accent," Dad said, when I told him. He can be pretty funny, sometimes.

And that gave me an idea.

CHAPTER SEVEN

X FACTOR HERE WE COME!

Our school was planning a talent show. I really wanted to be in it, but I didn't have a talent. The Trayches didn't either, unless you call being world class bullies, talent. Anyway, I got to thinking maybe the three of us could put on a skit. I already knew what I wanted to do if they'd go along with it, and if Mr. Flores would let us. I needed his permission to use Jorge.

When I told Howie and Homer my idea, I got the shock of my life. They thought it was awesome.

Howie even laughed. "I love that routine," he said. Homer agreed. (naturally)

They especially loved using Jorge. After we got Mr. Flores' permission, we started working on it at home. We you-tubed it to learn the words, but we changed them a little and shortened the skit some. The first time we practiced it at home, we got to laughing so hard we were falling all over ourselves. Mom and Dad laughed, too, even though they could hardly understand us. Joy liked it. She barked and wagged her tail.

"You boys had better practice a little self-control," Dad said, "or nobody will be able to fathom what you're saying."

That was going to be the tough part, all right.

We practiced for two weeks at home. We asked Mr. Flores if he'd teach Jorge some cue words at his house, so the parrot would answer right when we got to his part in the skit. We had one rehearsal at school and then the big day came. It was on a Saturday morning so parents could come. I was nervous, but we'd been through it so many times, I thought it'd go okay if Jorge didn't mess up.

Aunt Karen came and sat with my parents and Grandpa.

There were four kids ahead of us. Two sang, one played the viola, and the fourth did some magic tricks. Then it was our turn. Mr. Flores handed me Jorge's cage and gave us a thumbs up. This was it. I swallowed hard, and led the way onstage. We used the magician's card table to hold Jorge's cage. He was looking all around, his little head bobbing up and down. I had the microphone.

I cleared my throat. "Ladies and gentlemen, Howie and Homer Hall and I would like to present our version of the famous Bud Abbot and Lou Costello skit, 'Who's On First.' Since there are three of us, we divided Lou's part into two." I pointed to each of the twins. "Howie is 'Lou 1', Homer is 'Lou 2', and I'm Bud." I held the microphone over to Howie.

Howie: "Hey, Bud. I hear you're forming a new baseball team."
Me: "That's right. I'm the coach."
Homer: "Well if you're the coach, you must know all the players."
Me: "Yes, I certainly do."
Howie: "Well, I'd like to meet them. What are their names?"
Me: "Let's see. Who's on first, What's on second and I Don't Know's on third."
Homer: "That's what I want to find out."
Me: "I told you."
Howie: "You're the coach and you don't know the player's names?"

Me: "Well I should."

Homer: "Well then, *who's* on first?"

Me: "Yes."

Howie: "I mean the fella's name."

Me: "Who."

Homer: "The guy on first."

Me: "Who."

Howie: "The first baseman."

Me: "Who."

Homer: **"The guy playing…"**
         (Here's where Jorge comes in)
         Who! Who! Who! He screeched.

Me: "Right, Jorge, Who's on first."

Howie: "I am asking YOU who's on first."

Me: "That's the man's name."

Homer: "That's whose name?"

Me: "yes."

Howie: "Well, go ahead and tell me."

Me: "That's it."

Homer: "That's who?"

Me: "Yes."

Then Jorge lost it. Moving side to side on his little perch he squawked, "Uno dos tres quatro cinco seis."

This cracked the audience up even more. They were laughing their heads off, and so were we. Somehow we got through the rest of the skit. Then I took Jorge out of his cage and set him on my shoulder so he could bow to the audience. We'd practiced this at school.

"Gracias, Jorge," I said.

"Gracias!" he squawked, and pooped on my shoulder. Howie and Homer pointed at me and had a fit laughing. Homer was still giggling as he got Jorge off my shoulder and back in his cage. Then we made a fast exit.

There were five more acts, so we waited backstage until it was over and the judges made their decision. The other kids stood around looking anxious. We were, too, but we kept cracking up. Then Homer said, "Go get that poop off your shoulder. It's making me sick."

I couldn't believe I'd forgotten about it. Yuk! I went to the restroom and tried to get it off with a paper towel but it just smeared, so I took my shirt off. I held it under the faucet with the water on hard. I squeezed it out the best I could, but it was really cold against my skin. When I got back, the judges were announcing third place. Not us. Second place. Not us. Well, either we'd won or we weren't getting anything.

"And first prize goes to "Who's on First!"

We raced on stage with our fists in the air and got our prize. The Trayches couldn't stop smiling—especially since their dad was in town and had come and watched from the back. We were all over the place, we were so excited.

The prize was a gift certificate for free pizzas, so that's where we went afterwards. Aunt Karen and Uncle Henry went, too, but they didn't talk to each other. We kids laughed and re-enacted parts of the skit. Our parents laughed, too, and told us how proud they were of us.

When we finished eating, we all walked outside, still laughing and having fun. Aunt Karen hugged the boys and Uncle Henry patted them on the shoulder. Howie and Homer looked happy, but I watched their smiles fade as their parents walked across the parking lot in opposite directions and got into two separate cars.

CHAPTER EIGHT

"DAL-WRINKLE"

The next Saturday morning I was enjoying a wonderful weekend to myself, playing outside with Joy, when a car pulled up in front of the Hall's vacant house next door. Some people got out—a man, a lady, a girl and a little boy. The girl looked older than me, about twelve, I guessed. She was tall and had on a 'Lakers' baseball cap with a ponytail sticking out the back. The little kid looked about six. I was in the driveway with my basketball. Joy ran over there, barking and wagging her tail. The girl patted her and looked over at me and gave a sort of half wave. I sort of half waved back.

That afternoon, I went back outside to shoot some baskets and saw her banking shots off her garage door. The Halls had taken down their net and backboard when they sold the house.

I hollered at her, "Want to come over and shoot some?"

"Sure. Let me tell Mom," she said, running inside.

Here's where I show a Lakers fan what a Spurs fan can do!

She came over, and we played all afternoon. She told me her name was Andi (with an "i"), and I've got to tell you, she blew me away. She hardly ever missed a shot. And being so tall, she was tough to guard. So much for showing off for her!

At school, Monday morning, we had just gone to our desks, when Andi walked in. Wow. I thought she'd be in sixth grade. So, she's not older than me, just tall.

Mrs. Parks was back from being sick, and introduced her. "Class, this is Andrea Dalrymple." Andi leaned over to her and whispered something. "Excuse me," Mrs. Parks said. "It's Andi. She has just moved here from Los Angeles."

Dalrymple? If I know Howie, and I sure as heck do, he'll make something bad out of it.

Andi walked past me to a seat in the back. She smiled and punched me on the arm as she went by. I could hear Howie and Homer whispering behind me. Later, when the buzzer sounded for lunch, they were all over me.

"That your new girlfriend, Romeo?" Howie said, as we walked down the hall. "Is that what you've been doing while we're gone?"

Homer bumped into me—like he does to everything. "Yeah, you keeping her a secret, or something?"

"Guys, she moved into your old house on Saturday, and… I met her."

Howie stopped. "Our house? I thought those people had changed their minds. I hoped Mom and Dad would…." His shoulders slumped and he walked off by himself.

Homer was upset, too, but for a different reason. "A girl! In my room?"

"I don't know if she's in your room or not. She's got a little brother." *Sheesh! Those two.*

Next day after school the twins and I were home, shooting baskets and yelling at each other. Howie held the ball and stared next door with a scowl on his face. Andi was watching us from her driveway.

"Hi, come on over," I hollered.

"House stealer," Howie mumbled.

Andi ran over. "Hi," she said, to the guys.

I waited for them to say something, but they didn't. "This is Howie and Homer Hall," I said.

She smiled at them again. "I'm Andi Dalrymple."

"We know," Howie growled, throwing the ball hard at Homer. Homer was surprised and missed it. Andi ran and got it and threw it to me, and that was it—us against them. She was all over the place, dribbling, throwing, blocking. She dodged around Howie like he was hardly there, and threw over his head.

"They teach you to hog the court in LA, 'Dal-wrinkle?'" Howie razzed her.

Homer added his two cents. "Are all California girls giants, like you?"

Andi didn't answer them. She just played rings around them. Was that intense or what? 'Course she played rings around me, too. Humility time, for sure.

That Friday, after Howie and Homer left with their mom, Andi called across the yard and asked me if I'd come over and help her with something. Being the all American good guy that I am, I said sure.

When I walked into her room I couldn't believe my eyes. It was painted like a basketball court! On the three walls over her bed and desk and chest of drawers, she'd painted rows of seats, with people in them, and the aisles in between had little bitty men selling hotdogs and peanuts and pennants. Down the other end from her bed, over her closet, was a basketball net—a *real* one—and a scoreboard painted in one corner. Her ceiling slanted up from the walls in a big rectangle, so there was room to actually throw the ball. It was truly awesome.

"Did you paint all this, yourself?" I asked.

She smiled, looking around the room. "Mom and I have been working on it all week. She's a commercial artist."

"Looks like you're an artist, too," I said.

"Thanks. It was fun. But now I need you to help me measure for the lines on the floor."

She was going to paint the floor? Wow. Her mother joined us with a big tape measure.

She and I held it stretched across the floor against the baseboards, while Andy marked with a pencil. Then we put red and black tape on the lines.

"Easier than paint," she said.

"And we don't mark up the floor," added her mom.

All of a sudden I thought of something. "Andi, if my Grandpa says it's okay, would you paint a ranch scene on one wall of my bedroom at his house? I'll furnish the paint."

"Sure. That'd be fun. You tell me what you want, and I'll draw a picture of it first so you can see what it'd look like, and if you'd like to add anything."

"Awesome! I'll ask him and let you know." I looked around her room again. "Boy, the Trayches would flip over this if they could see it."

"The who?" Andi asked.

I explained my name for my temporary house "puests" and told her the whole story about why they were there.

Andi listened. "I get it, now," she said. "That explains a lot."

"Yeah, it's sad, but they've been bullies forever. I felt sorry for them, too, and now I've got them living with me until school's over."

"Well, at least you have weekends," she said. "It could be worse."

"I guess. But summer can't come too soon for me."

CHAPTER NINE

VALENTINE'S

February means giving valentines (gag). I made myself a promise: if I couldn't find any funny ones for school, I was going to make some, myself. I hate all that mushy "BE MINE" stuff. I don't know why we have to have Valentine's Day anyway. The one good thing is cupcakes. Somebody's mom always brings some. And they're usually pretty good, too, with icing and M&M's and stuff. One time, though, Herbert Baumgardner's mom brought bran muffins with raisins. I almost puked!

On Saturday, Andi and I were playing basketball and talking about school and stuff, and all of a sudden she said, "I'm having a Valentine's party next Saturday. Want to come?"

"Why?"

"Why what?"

"Why are you having a Valentine's party?"

She laughed. "You think we're going to dance or something? You don't have to dress up or wear red, or anything."

"Okay... but why?"

Andi looked at me like I was her little brother. "Travis, do you mean why am I having a party? Or why am I having a Valentine's party?"

"Yeah. Both."

"Okay. It's my birthday, and Mom thought I could invite a few kids from school for a party. And since it's almost Valentine's, we thought that would be a good theme."

"Theme?"

"Forget it, Travis. You want to come, or not?"

"Sure. 'Course you'll have to have the Trayches, too."

"I know. That's okay."

I told Howie and Homer about it when they got back from their weekend.

"That's a dumb idea!" Howie said. "What do you do at a Valentine's party, anyway, make up poems? Have to kiss girls?"

Homer thought that was hilarious. "Yeah. Roses are red, violets are blue, I'm sure as heck not gonna kiss you."

Howie joined in. "Roses are red, violets are blue, I can play basketball better than you."

"Yeah, right." I snorted. "Well, I'm going whether you guys go or not."

"Hey, we didn't say we weren't going." Howie growled.

I got out of there before there was an argument. I wish, just once, they'd come up with a positive thought. One positive thought! Is that asking too much? 'Course I didn't tell them I agreed with them that a Valentine's party was a dumb idea.

Monday, after school, Andi brought three invitations over. She had drawn them herself.

On the front there were kids playing with hearts—throwing them into a basketball net, playing badminton with them and juggling them. Underneath it said, "Come to my Valentine birthday party," and inside it had the date and stuff in red. I had told Mom about her room and her favorite team, so we bought her a Lakers T-shirt from the three of us.

The day before Andi's party was our class Valentine's party. I made my own valentines. I liked the first one I thought up best, but Mom wouldn't let me take it. It showed a stick figure boy with a big circle head and his mouth open, leaning over the toilet, with hearts pouring out of his mouth. I thought it was pretty funny. It sure showed how I felt about valentines.

"Draw something nice, Travis," Mom said, "or we'll go get some."

"Esta bien," I said. Mr. Flores taught us that. It means that's good, or okay.

I ended up drawing a stick figure holding a big Valentine box of candy on the front. You turn to the inside and the box is empty. Underneath it says, "It's the thought that counts. I thought you'd like the box. Ha Ha." Everybody got the same one. I made copies.

Howie and Homer were original. They cut out hearts from red construction paper they'd folded several times, and wrote "Guess Who?" on the back. I hated to admit it, but that was pretty smart. It only took them about ten minutes, start to finish. They liked my first try, though—the kid barfing valentines—that cracked them up. I sent it to Grandpa.

The next day was Andi's party. I decided I'd wear red even though she said I didn't have to. Actually it was my favorite shirt I wore a lot, anyway. The weather was sunny and warm—February in San Antonio—sometimes.

Andi had taped the outline of a big heart on the garage door with red tape. Then a smaller one inside it, and a smaller one inside that. There was a black 10 in the center of the smallest heart, a 5 on the rim of the next biggest heart, and a 1 on the rim of the outside heart. She handed out long plastic tubes to everybody, with their names on them—so nobody would get anybody else's germs, I guess. That must have been her mom's idea. There were three rubber tipped darts. Everybody got three turns, and the highest scorer won, of course.

We blew the three darts, then went to the back of the line, until we'd all had three turns.

We had "sword" fights while we waited. 'Least, the boys did.

Next, we had a scavenger hunt in the back yard. It's a real big yard with lots of plants and hedges. We had a list of things to find, like a comb, red plastic scissors, a yellow tennis ball—stuff like that. Whoever found the most things on the list got a prize. Mrs. D. kept having to stop Andi's little brother, Charlie, from showing the kids where things were. He must have helped hide them. He thought he was pretty funny.

I found the tennis ball, and Andi said I could give it to Joy.

Everybody was counting the items they'd found. "Can we count ours together since we're twins?" Howie asked.

Mrs. D. thought he was joking, and laughed. He wasn't, though. I could tell.

After the prize was given, which was two tickets to the movies (I didn't win), we went inside for birthday cake. It was a heart shaped cake, naturally—chocolate with white icing.

There were red icing hearts all over it with "red-hots" in the middle of them. Hot, but good.

Andi and her mom made it. I was beginning to wonder if there was anything Andi couldn't do.

After that we played dodge ball in the driveway until kids started leaving. When everybody had gone except us, I asked Andi if she would let Howie and Homer see her room.

She said sure, and led the way upstairs. You should have seen the Trayches' eyes when they walked through her door.

"Andi and her mom painted it themselves," I said.

Homer was bug-eyed. "Wo-o-ow!"

Howie just scowled.

When we got home, Homer said, "Man, I was picturing pink curtains and girl stuff. That was awesome."

Howie kicked the door frame and went and flopped on his bed.

"I thought you'd want to see it," I said. "Didn't you think it was neat?"

He glared at me. "What's so neat about a room that used to be yours and now it belongs to somebody else?"

I glared back. "Yeah, tell me about it."

Howie looked away. "But you'll get yours back."

Yeah, in three months, fifteen days and three hours! Believe me, I've been counting.

CHAPTER TEN

HELP!

It seemed like I was going backwards instead of forward. Every time I thought maybe I was getting along better with the Trayches, they'd do something to make me mad. Or they'd do something really stupid. Usually both. And I'd lose it.

Listen to their latest stunt. Aunt Karen had given them a big box of gum balls for Valentine's. I was looking for Joy the other night after supper and heard all this laughing from their room. I went in. They were feeding her gum balls! They rolled them across the floor, and Joy chased and ate them. I don't know how many she'd had, but I grabbed her collar and pulled her out of there, calling them every horrible name I could think of.

Mom heard me, of course.

"Travis, you are grounded for a week!"

I was really mad. I stood there, shaking. Why didn't she say something to the Trayches? I could hear Howie laughing because I'd been grounded. I exploded. "Well, our perfect house guests just fed Joy a whole bunch of gum balls, the stupid jerks. I get grounded, and the ghouls from the Underworld get nothing. Not fair! Not fair, Mom." I was crying by then. "Sometimes I think you and Dad forget who your real son is."

"Travis, that's not true, and you know it. But I can't have you talking like …"

I ran into my room. "And by the way, Joy's going to be sick, you know!"

And she was, big time. In the middle of the night. On my bed. Ekkkk! I thought I'd be sick, too.

Mom got up and took care of it, because I sure couldn't.

Turns out she did have a talk with the twins, but I was still grounded. And they weren't. I kept Joy away from them. Even if she had gotten sick from the gum balls, it didn't mean she wouldn't eat more if the twins gave them to her. And they just might. It's like living with criminals. And now Mom's mad at me, and I'm mad at Mom! And Dad.

All this time I've been trying to be nice to the twins, and put myself in their shoes, but why should I? They're not nice to me. They stick together, and Homer does whatever Howie does. Here they are, living in *my* house—in *my* room—and acting like I'm not even here.

I know I have (or had) a happy family, and they don't. And that makes a difference. But I'll tell you, they've been the same as long as I've known them, always picking on somebody, and making fun of some poor kid, and mad about everything, it seemed. It's a big job trying to get along with them. I don't know if I can do it.

CHAPTER ELEVEN

AWESOME, AWESOME, AWESOME!

I had the absolute best birthday in the whole world! In the whole galaxy! Grandpa got three tickets to a Spurs game and told me I could ask a friend. I asked Andi. She was as excited as I was even though they weren't playing the Lakers.

Grandpa knew I hadn't been looking forward to my birthday too much because I didn't want to have a party. The Trayches would've found a way to ruin it and there was no way I could have a party without them. So, he got us tickets. We had hotdogs and popcorn and cold drinks and yelled and cheered—the noise in the AT&T Center was so loud we could hardly hear each other—and I had the best time ever in my eleven years! My hero, Tim Duncan was awesome! And the Spurs won!

And then... I still can't believe it...after the game, Tim came over and hand-bumped me and gave me an autographed basketball! And wished me happy birthday! Awesome times 1000!

Grandpa arranged it. He called the Spurs office and made the request, and Tim said he'd do it. What a great guy! And what a great grandpa! Birthdays don't get any better than that.

Howie and Homer just about croaked when they saw my signed basketball. Which I will keep forever!

CHAPTER TWELVE

HOWIE'S SURPRISE

About two weeks later Andi came jogging around to the back patio where I was feeding Joy. The twins were swinging in the hammock, laughing at some joke they'd pulled on somebody. She was all excited. "Guess what? Dad says I can have a tree house! And not just a normal tree house, either, one with different levels—a double decker! And we're going to build it together." She stood there, grinning.

For the first time ever, Howie and Homer and I had the same thought at the same time. "Can I help?" we blurted.

Andi's grin faded. "Well, um,…I guess. I'll ask him," she said, turning to go. Then she stopped, and fixed us with this killer look. "But, guys, it's *my* tree house. Got it? What I say goes."

"Right," I said.

Homer nodded. "Okay."

Howie stuck out his chin. "The tree was ours, first. We should have some say."

Andi sighed. "Howie, I'll tell you what. If you come up with a good idea, we'll try to use it."

That seemed to be okay with him. At least, he didn't say anything else. For once.

This was going to be so awesome. The oak tree in their side yard between our two houses was perfect for a tree house. It had big, thick limbs that were close enough together to climb from one to the other, and we *had* climbed it a lot, but a tree house! With floors on different levels! I couldn't wait!

~ ~ ~

"So, you boys want to help?" Mr. Dalrymple said. He had a pencil stuck behind his ear.

"Yes, sir," we chimed, together.

We followed him to his workshop out in the garage where there were all kinds of power tools, jars of nails and screws, and saws and hammers hanging on the wall. Everything was up on pegboards and on shelves. Ultra neat. He showed us the level and right angle and other stuff we'd be using.

We studied the plans he'd drawn, and he asked us if we had any ideas or comments. I thought they were perfect just like they were. I guess Howie thought so, too.

"How about a pulley," Andi suggested, "so we can bring up food and stuff—in a bucket or something." We agreed with that, for sure.

Howie and Homer got to help that first week, which was mostly measuring and sawing. I had my new Christmas camera and took some good pictures of Mr. D. showing us how to do stuff, and everybody working. There was a ton of lumber, and he double-checked the measurements and made us do it, too.

One day while we were marking the tree with yellow chalk where the boards would be attached, he said, "Kids, I suggest you put the ladder boards on the side of the tree away from the street."

"Why?" Andi asked.

"Because then you won't be advertising the fact that you have your private club house up there."

Sounded reasonable.

On weekdays, after Mr. D. got home, we didn't actually have that much time to work on it. And Andi had piano and soccer practice two of the days, so we didn't get a lot done that first week. Then it was the weekend and the Halls left, so it was just Andi, her dad, and me. I liked that. Having the Trayches gone on the weekends gave me a little of my old life back. I was really tired of them being around all the time.

Mr. D. gave me some safety goggles and watched closely as I used the electric saw. We stacked the steps, rails, and flooring boards in separate piles in the garage.

The second Friday, after school, Howie got out his overnight bag and just stood there looking at it. "I don't want to leave," he said. "I want to stay here and work on the tree house. You guys will finish it before we get back."

"Me, too," said Homer.

Oh, no! Give me a break!

"You need to ask your mother," Mom said. "I bet she'd miss having you with her."

"Yeah, I bet she would, too," I added.

They called, and she said they could stay until the tree house was finished if they wanted to. Of course she said yes. Of course she did. I bet they'd never had anybody say no to them in their whole slimy, ogre lives.

~ ~ ~

"Okay, everybody," Mr. D. said. "Time to start on the platforms."

One at a time we lifted the boards up into the tree. That didn't leave much room for us to work, but we managed. We had to be sure we made the floors level. That was the hardest part. And we nailed. Boy, did we nail. None of us had had much experience, and it wasn't as easy as we'd thought. We hit a lot in crooked, and Howie whacked his thumb and threw the hammer. It hit me in the leg and he didn't even apologize. Andi's dad sent him home.

Nobody, and I mean *nobody* can ruin a perfectly good mood like Howie Hall. When I got home he was holed up in his room. Fine. He could stay there forever.

The next day when Howie showed up with us to work on the tree house, Andi's dad asked him if he had his temper under control. Howie's face tightened up, but he said, "Yes, sir."

A little later I saw Mr. D. show Howie how to strike the nail without bending it. "You've got the strength, Howie," he said. "Just hit it solid. That's the way."

On the third Saturday we finished building, and Mr. D. loaded us all in his car to go to a sporting goods store.

"What are we going for, Dad?" Andi asked, hopping in next to him.

"Something neat," he said. "I just thought of it last night."

When we were almost there, Mr. D. looked at us in the rear view mirror. "How would you guys like to be invisible?" We grinned at each other. Mr. D. grinned back. "I take it that's a yes," he said.

When we got there, we walked down the aisles, all excited, wondering what in the world Mr. D. had in mind. Back in the hunting department he found what he was looking for—some grayish-brown canvas webbing with spaces in between.

"If we hang it from the rails on the street side," he said, "it'll hide the wood, and nobody can see inside. Air can get through so it won't be so hot. And if I'm right about the color, it ought to blend pretty much with the bark. And voila! A secret clubhouse."

Sweet! Nobody walking by would even know we were up there. And right then, I knew I wanted it to be a super-spy safe house. I'd have to think of a neat code name.

When we got back to the tree house, we took turns with the power stapler. The webbing was pretty close to the color of the bark, and it looked awesome.

Mrs. D. came out with some lemonade for everybody. We stretched out on the grass and looked up at the tree. I don't know about them, but I was pretty proud of that tree house.

"Cool, huh?" Andi said. "Let's give it a name. What do you think of 'Sherwood Forest?' Remember how Robin Hood's men all hid up in the trees?"

*Well, it **is** her tree house. Goodbye, super spies.*

We lay there, letting that idea soak in, thinking about Robin Hood and Little John and all the rest of them up in the trees.

All of a sudden Howie said, "You'd have to be Maid Marian."

Andi popped up. "Fat chance! I'll be Robin Hood."

"I'm not taking orders from a girl Robin Hood," Howie shot back.

He was doing it again. Ruining everything. I jumped up. "Howie, why don't you just…"

Homer interrupted. "Hey, listen. What about a hunting lodge like in Africa? I saw an ad one time on the Internet for this hunting lodge that had rooms up in trees."

Wow. That almost made me forget Howie, and my own idea, but I said it, anyway, just to get it out there. "What about a super-spy safe house, and our code name could be 'The Undetectables'?"

Andi smiled. "Great ideas, guys! Let's take a vote. "

"Hey, wait a minute," Howie said, leaning up on his elbow. "*I* have an idea."

Everybody looked at him like "yeah, right."

He looked at Andi. "When your dad asked if we'd like to be invisible, it reminded me of those 'No-See-ums' at the coast—you know, those little stinging bugs? We could call ourselves 'The No-See-ums', and meet in our invisible tree house. And"…he looked at me with a raised eyebrow, "it could still be a super-spy safe house."

Would you believe it? *Two* positive thoughts!

CHAPTER THIRTEEN

SPRING BREAK

"Do you ever hear from your dad?" I asked Howie. We were sitting on the sofa watching TV after supper—he at one end, me at the other. It was a commercial. Homer was stretched out on the rug with his eyes closed.

"Nah," Howie said, like it didn't matter.

I couldn't believe this. Uncle Henry had seemed like he cared a lot, last time I saw him, which I guess was right after the skit. "Where is he?" I asked.

Homer raised up from the floor. "He's in Colorado, working for a mountain resort. And we *have* heard from him, twice."

"Mom has, not us," Howie said.

"He *asked* about us."

"Big deal."

A picture of snow-covered mountains popped into my head. "Wow! You guys will get to go skiing! And this summer you could go white water rafting and fishing and hiking and stuff!"

I was getting all excited for them. And a little envious.

Howie shook his head. "He doesn't want us."

"You don't know that!" Homer shouted, throwing a sofa pillow at him. "Stop saying that!"

Howie jumped up off the sofa and leaned down in his brother's face. "How many phone calls have *you* gotten? Or Spring Break or summer invitations?"

Homer just glared at him.

"Right," Howie said, and stomped off to his room.

That night when Mom came in to say goodnight, I told her what had happened.

"Oh Sweetie," she said, giving me a hug. "That is so sad. Maybe I'll call Aunt Karen and see if she can do something." Then she straightened up. "Or, maybe I'll just call their dad. After all, he left his kids in our care."

"Good for you, Mom. But I'm glad *I* don't have to call him and get in an argument."

"I have no intention of arguing with him, Travis. But I do have an idea. What if I tell him that since we haven't heard from him about any plans of his own, we'd like to take the boys to the coast with us for Spring Break? Maybe he'll feel guilty and invite them to visit him."

At first I was excited about going to the coast, then it crashed through what she'd said.

"Mom, please! I don't want them on my Spring Break! I've been looking forward to a break from them! Don't you ever want to be with me without them?"

Mom reached out to hug me, but I backed away.

She sighed. "Travis, your Aunt Karen is working and Uncle Henry hasn't asked them. What do you suggest?"

"You could tell him you're sure he wants his kids for Spring Break, and we've got our own plans." Sounded reasonable to me.

"You'd have someone to do things with if they went," she said.

"I've got other friends I could take, Mom. Real friends."

"A minute ago you were all for me calling their dad."

"Yeah, call him and tell him to take them for awhile. That's what they want." *And it's sure as heck what I want!*

~ ~ ~

Well, guess what? They're going with us. Whoo-pee. Uncle Henry sent some money.

He never said a word about the twins coming to see him.

One afternoon right before we left, Mom said "Okay, boys, let's go to the library and get some books for the trip."

Howie shook his head. "No, thanks." Homer didn't say anything.

Mom looked at them for a minute. "You guys have seen the Harry Potter movies and Indiana Jones, right?"

"Sure," Homer said. "They're awesome."

Mom smiled. "Well, they were awesome books first. Come on. Last one in the car gets to do the laundry tonight."

Yikes! We all hopped in.

At the library, the guys and I went to the mid-grade section and Mom went off to the adult. I got another Gary D. Schmidt book. I love his books. Howie picked one of Brian Anderson's Zack Proton books. Homer wanted a dog book. Mom came back and found *The Call of the Wild* for him.

~ ~ ~

We went down to Port Aransas and stayed at this place right on the beach. After we unloaded the car, we put on sun screen, mostly just hitting our noses and shoulders. Howie squirted some down the back of my bathing suit, and I got him in the head. Ha! Then we were off, screaming and yelling. Dad followed, lugging two beach chairs and a cooler. Mom came out later with towels and a Frisbee.

Joy was so happy she was jumping around and barking and ran straight for the water. We stayed out all afternoon, diving in the waves, making drip sand castles, and playing Frisbee. Joy loved the Frisbee. She was a good catcher, and she always brought it back.

Finally Mom asked if we were hungry. Silly question. We raced back to the condo. Dad pointed to the bathroom. "Showers first, guys."

We grouched, but we were hungry. Mom had brought some fried chicken for our first night's meal. My favorite parts are the wings, and since nobody else wanted them I got them both and a thigh. Grandpa calls the thigh the second joint. I've always wondered what's the first joint? But I keep forgetting to ask him.

While we ate, Mom checked the tide schedule and said, "Looks like the tide will be out in the morning. How would you boys like to catch some crabs for supper?"

The twins shrugged. Not exactly enthusiastic.

"It's fun," I said. *Or it could be.*

Early next morning we ate a quick breakfast and drove to the jetty. We had some chicken necks Mom had brought, pieces of wood with string wrapped around them and a net. I had my camera in my pants pocket. Dad handed us each wood and string and told Howie and Homer to tie the loose end of the string around a chicken neck.

"Hold up the necks, guys," I said. I got some good pictures of them with Dad, in his old fishing hat with lures on it, demonstrating chicken-neck-tying. Then we stretched out on our stomachs and dropped our lines. And waited.

I told the guys that if they caught a crab to get it in the net quick before it saw them or it would let lose. They thought that was funny.

"You're just making that up," Howie sneered.

"Just telling you. See for yourself."

Sure enough, the first one Howie caught he pulled it up too high and Joy saw it and went bazurk, barking. The crab dropped off.

"Stupid dog made me lose my crab!" Howie yelled.

Dad stood up. "Howie, let's take a walk, son.

Howie shook his head.

"Come on. I want to tell you something."

They walked off down the jetty.

I don't know what Dad said, but in a little while they were back and Howie lay down on his stomach and mumbled, "I'm sorry."

To give myself credit, I didn't say anything. During the morning we caught some and lost some, but ended up more caught than lost. At twelve, Dad said he thought we had enough. We took them to show Mom, pretty proud of ourselves.

"You guys did great!" Mom said, pouring us some limeade. Then she got out a big soup pot, filled it with water and put it on the stove to boil. We stood there watching as she added some seasoning called crab-boil. As it heated, the smell got so strong it made us cough and our eyes water. Whew! Lots of spices.

Howie sputtered, "What are you trying to do to those crabs, sanitize them?"

Have to admit that was pretty funny.

When the water boiled, Dad came over and dumped our crabs in. The twins and I watched as they turned red. Their dying bubbles floated to the top.

"Sorry, guys," Homer said. "Wow, I bet that hurts."

Howie snorted. "Yeah, I bet one of them is Mr. Crabs from SpongeBob. So long, Mr.Crabs. We're going to make a crabby patty out of *you*."

Another funny. Sometimes I think Howie has two people inside him. If he weren't so mad all the time he could be fun. Maybe.

After they were cooked, Mom recruited us—even Dad—to help clean them. Howie grumbled under his breath, "Geez, we caught 'em. Now we gotta clean 'em, too?"

"I'll tell you what," Mom said. "I'll give you boys a dollar for each crab you clean, but you've got to do it right. Watch and I'll show you how to get all the meat out. Wash your hands first."

Cleaning crabs is a lot of work and really messy. Some of the meat is in these little hard-to-get-to places. And sometimes the shells cut your fingers. After we'd each cleaned two, the guys and I agreed it wasn't worth another dollar to clean any more. Mom thanked us for our efforts and pushed six messy hands into a sink of hot, soapy water.

Dad took us to get hamburgers while Mom stayed there making crabcakes. When we got back, she had saved some crabmeat in a little bowl of melted butter for us to taste. Oh, man was it good! I could've eaten ten times that much. Howie and Homer hesitated, at first. I said they didn't have to try it. All the more for me. So, of course they did. They loved it.

Dad sat at the table, checking his tackle box. "You boys are excellent crabbers," he said.

"And cleaners," Homer added, grinning.

"And cleaners," Dad agreed. He stood up, reached in his pocket and got out his wallet. "Don't seem to have any ones, but I do happen to have three fives." he said, handing them out. "That's for a great job, catching and cleaning. Want to go fishing tomorrow?"

"Yes, sir!" we said, together.

Then Howie asked, "Do we have to clean fish, too?"

"Only the ones you catch," Dad said. "You catch a lot of fish, you clean a lot of fish. Unless you're partial to scales and innards."

Dad, the comedian.

Howie, the lazy. Howie, the griper. Howie, the ruin everything-er!

CHAPTER FOURTEEN

THE CALL

S pring Break went by like we'd fast forwarded it. The Trayches came back happy. Why shouldn't they be? They had a new family. Mine!

I did have fun some of the time, but I wish my real friends had been there. It seemed like my parents paid more attention to Howie and Homer than they did to me. It probably wouldn't have been as bad if the twins had been friendlier to me. But they hardly even spoke to me unless they had to.

I guess one good thing from the trip is the twins are eating everything Mom fixes now, and it sure makes her happy. I think trying crabmeat and fish opened up a whole new food world for them. And they found out some other good stuff they'd been missing, like carrots—Mom fixes them real good with butter, sugar and cinnamon, and Dad's grilled chicken and veggies. Yum!

Grandpa came over to stay with us the other night when Mom and Dad went out, and he couldn't believe it was the same two boys. He pulled me aside after supper. "I think aliens have invaded their bodies. You better watch out. They'll be eating the woodwork next."

Grandpa, the kidder.

I asked him what he thought about Andi painting a ranch scene on one wall in my bedroom at his house, and he said it was okay with him. In fact he thought it was a great idea.

I've been trying to decide what I want.

When we were in the kitchen cleaning up from supper, he said, "How'd it go with the twins down at the coast?"

They were watching TV, of course. Not helping.

"I think Mom and Dad would adopt them if they could," I grumbled.

"Aw, Travis, you know better than that."

"I'm not kidding. Sometimes I wonder if they'd even notice if I left."

"Yeah, their grocery bill would go down, considerably."

"Very funny, Grandpa."

"Well, why don't you tell me about it?"

I know he was trying to help, but if there was one thing I didn't want to talk about it was my vacation with the twins. I looked up at him. "Nothing's going to change until they leave, and that won't be any time soon. So it sure won't do any good to talk about it."

"Well, then, let's talk about you."

"Me? The invisible son? Grandpa, Mom and Dad are so busy making the Trayches feel good, they don't take up for me at all about anything." I put the dish towel up and went to find Joy.

A few nights after we were back I heard Howie on the phone with his mom. He was telling her more stuff about the coast, and every other word—or every two words—were "Travis' dad."

It wasn't long after that, maybe a couple of days, when "the call" came. We were eating supper and Mom answered the phone.

"Well, hello, Henry. We're fine, thanks, and you? Yes, they are, but I'm afraid you caught us in the middle of supper."

Homer jumped up from the table and raced to the phone. Mom waved her hand at him.

"That's all right," she continued. "Give me your number, and the boys will call you when they've finished."

Howie and Homer looked like human vacuum cleaners—whoosh! I don't think they even chewed. Mom told them to take the phone back in their room, so they'd have some privacy.

"Guess what?" Howie said, bouncing into the dining room a few minutes later. Homer was grinning. "Dad asked us if we wanted to come to Colorado this summer!"

"That's terrific, Howie," Dad said. Mom got up and gave them both a hug.

That night in bed I got to thinking. What made their dad call all of a sudden? Then I remembered Mr. Dalrymple teaching them to build a tree house, and my dad teaching them to crab and cast a line. And the pictures the twins sent to their dad of themselves with the other dads doing these things. So, you know what I think? I think Uncle Henry is jealous. How about that? Maybe he'll take his kids back.

CHAPTER FIFTEEN

SUBCONCIOUS EVIL EYE?

I should have known it was too good to last. We hadn't been home from the coast a week, and Howie was back to his old sarcastic self. I guess he felt he wasn't the center of attention any more. And he just flat didn't like Andi. We were shooting baskets in my driveway. Andi got the ball away from him and made a slam dunk.

Howie grabbed the ball. "You think you're so great, don't you, 'Stilts'? You planning to try out for the Spurs?"

"Shut up, Howie," I said.

"Make me!" he yelled, shoving me into the garage door.

Andi's face was red and she was mad. "Howie, what is your problem? Why can't you act like a normal human being, for once?"

"Because he's not!" I growled, shoving him back. "He's got 'jerk' programmed in his brain. It'll probably be there forever."

Howie sneered. "Well, I'll be out of your hair tomorrow, 'whiney-pants'. Good old Friday."

I walked off. "I can't wait! Come on, Andi."

Homer spoke up. "Hey, come back, guys, we were having fun."

"See you tomorrow, Travis," Andi said, heading back to her house.

I wondered if Homer said anything to his brother about ruining the game after I went inside. I hoped he had.

I was fed up with Howie's temper. Andi didn't deserve his ugly comments. She'd been nothing but nice to him. I didn't speak to him after that. Not that night or the next day, which was Friday. And when they left with their mom after school, I didn't even say goodbye.

Saturday morning Andi and I were playing basketball, when Mom came outside. She motioned for us to come in the house.

"Sit down, kids, please."

I knew it was something bad from the look on her face. I felt a heavy weight in my stomach.

She motioned us to the sofa and sat between us. "I'm afraid I have some terrible news. Aunt Karen just called from the hospital. Howie got hit by a car this morning." She put her arms around us and hugged us both. "He's in a coma."

I felt numb. I couldn't believe it.

"Is he going to be all right?" Andi asked in a shaky voice.

Mom put her cheek on Andi's head. "We don't know yet. It's too soon to tell."

Andi started crying. Then she pulled away and ran out of the house.

I looked up at Mom. "How did it happen?"

"He ran out in the street after his basketball. The car couldn't stop in time."

Horrible pictures flashed through my mind of Howie flying through the air, Howie lying bloody in the street. I closed my eyes and held Mom tight.

As soon as Dad got back from the hardware store, we went to the hospital to be with Aunt Karen and Homer.

Howie was in PICU—pediatric intensive care unit—so we couldn't go in. But his room was the first one by the nurses' station, and his curtain was open, so we could see him through the window in the door. His head was all bandaged up and there was a wide, white collar around his neck. His face was a mess—swollen and purple. His right arm was in a cast, and he had tubes everywhere—in his other arm and coming out of his nose. He looked terrible!

Homer was standing next to his mom, staring at his brother. He looked like he was in pain, too. Dad poked his head in and asked a nurse to get them to come out in the hall. When they did, Dad put his arm around Homer's shoulder, and Mom hugged her sister for a long time. Aunt Karen's eyes were all red. I'd never seen a grownup look that scared before. It was awful.

I stared at Howie, too, through the window, feeling scared, myself. And guilty. Was there something down in my subconscious mind? Something… bad? You know how in books and movies when somebody's mad at somebody else, and they don't say goodbye to that person, and then something bad happens to that person? And the person who didn't say goodbye feels guilty, like whatever happened was their fault? That's how I felt.

Homer looked so out of it I asked him if he'd like to come back with us, but he just shook his head.

After we left, Mom told us Homer had seen it happen. He was really shaken, and was going to stay with his mom until they knew more about Howie's condition. I couldn't imagine seeing something that terrible happen to your own brother and not be able to do anything about it.

Grandpa asked Joy and me to spend the weekend with him. I told him how guilty I felt and why. He sat me down at the supper table and talked to me while we ate baby back ribs.

"Son, I'm not sayin' we're not responsible for what we say, because we are. You be clear in your head about that." He looked up at me and licked sauce from his fingers. "But I *am* saying there's no way on God's green earth you are responsible for what happened to Howie, whether you told him goodbye or not. It's true, though, that you two boys have been at each other's throats for so long you don't seem to know when to quit. So I'll tell you, straight. Now's the time."

He was right. I knew the fights Howie and I'd had weren't all his fault, and I still felt bad about what I'd said about his brain.

After supper we ate Blue Bell Homemade Vanilla ice cream and watched the John Wayne movie, "True Grit." Joy was on the sofa with me, and Grandpa was stretched out in his chair with his feet on the ottoman. He looked over at me. "It don't get much better'n this, does it, boy?"

I love my Grandpa.

~ ~ ~

Three days later Howie came out of his coma. Thank goodness! I was so happy for Homer and Aunt Karen. My first thought though, after being thankful of course, was that I bet now that Howie was awake he could really feel the pain. He was hurt in so many places. I guess they had him on super pain meds, though. But I hoped they didn't let him see himself. Not for a while, anyway.

That afternoon Aunt Karen brought Homer back to our house. She said he'd missed two days of school already, and he needed to go back. He didn't want to because his dad had come and he wanted to be with him. I felt really bad for him.

The next afternoon, which was Wednesday, Homer wanted to shoot some baskets. We played hard. I think he needed to get some anger out of his system. Or fear. Maybe he just needed to *do* something. "That felt good," he said, afterwards. At least his face wasn't so ghost-white anymore.

His mom called him every night with a report. Howie was speaking, she said, but his speech was slow and slurred. The doctor didn't know yet how long that would last or the extent of damage to his brain. Howie was going to start speech therapy.

I tried to believe what Grandpa told me, but the weight in my stomach was getting heavier.

CHAPTER SIXTEEN

BIG MOUTH!

The No-See-Ums met in our secret safe house, without our fourth member. We climbed up to the top level, where the leaves were blowing around and just sat there, not knowing what to say. It was peaceful without Howie. I wondered if they were thinking that, too… and if they felt guilty for thinking it, like I did.

"How's Howie doing?" I asked Homer.

"He's been moved to a private room," he said, but he didn't sound like that was good news.

Andi smiled. "That's great. Let's make him a card."

We agreed, and she climbed down and got some paper and one of those lap cushion desk things. She drew a picture of the three of us with a bubble over each head, and the word "Howie" in each bubble, to show him we were thinking about him. Then she wrote, "Get well soon," and we signed it.

"Let's send him a card every week," she suggested. "I'll work on some pictures."

I liked that. "Good idea."

Homer just sat there, tearing up a leaf.

The next Monday, after Homer came back from the weekend with his mother, Andi and I told him we'd like to go visit Howie.

"He doesn't want to see you," he said.

Andi frowned. "Neither one of us? Not even Travis?"

"No."

"Why not?" I asked. "Is he still mad?"

"No, he… he just doesn't."

I bet he's still mad at me.

That night when Mom sat on my bed, I asked her if she knew why Howie didn't want to see us.

She straightened the sheet across my chest. "Aunt Karen says he's having a hard time. He can't make words sound right, and he's embarrassed. He doesn't want to see anybody except his family."

"But I'm family. And Andi and I could maybe make him laugh and feel better."

"He doesn't feel like laughing, Travis. Put yourself in his place. Would you?"

No, I sure as heck wouldn't. But I've got to do *something* for him. I should never have said he had "jerk" programmed in his brain forever. Or that his brain was lopsided like his ears. Oh-h-h, me and my big, stupid mouth!

CHAPTER SEVENTEEN

SECRETS IN THE DARK

There's good news and bad news.

The good news is Uncle Henry wants to get back together with his family. Homer says he and Howie are happy about it. Aunt Karen said she was willing to give it a try. I think it's awesome. Uncle Henry wants them to move to Colorado as soon as Howie can travel.

The bad news is Howie's still slurring his words and reacting slowly to questions, Mom says. I guess the speech therapy is going to take a long time. She also said Uncle Henry was very upset over the accident and was blaming himself for not being there with his family. Looks like I'm not the only one feeling guilty.

Homer is still going to stay with us until the end of the school year, which is two months away. 'Course, that was the plan anyway.

I'll have to say, Homer is a different person when Howie's not around. I guess when you're a twin, you don't get much chance to be by yourself. Right now, though, he's a mixture of being happy about his parents, and worried about his brother.

I've been thinking. Since I don't know how to make it up to Howie for calling him names—I mean I can't even see him—maybe I can at least help Homer feel better and have some fun before he leaves. Maybe we could even be friends.

~ ~ ~

Weeks went by. Homer and Andi and I had fun together. Homer started talking more, and it wasn't sarcastic like it used to be. He didn't come out and apologize to Andi for the things he'd said before, but you could tell he was doing it by the way he acted toward her.

One night after supper Homer and I were still in the kitchen when Dad walked in with his guitar. Mom was working at her desk in the sitting room.

"You boys got a request?" he asked, tuning the strings. While we were thinking, he started playing "The Streets of Laredo." Dad and I were singing away, and I elbowed Homer. "Come on, sing."

He shook his head.

"Streets of Laredo" has a zillion verses, so Dad stopped when we couldn't remember any more words and played "I'm an Old Cowhand, from the Rio Grande." I guess Homer changed his mind, or maybe he just knew the words to this one. Yikes! I'd forgotten he couldn't carry a tune. Dad and I sang louder and louder, trying to drown him out. Joy howled.

Mom walked in waving a patient's chart she was working on from the pediatric clinic. "Shoo!" she said. "You cowpokes go outside and sing to the coyotes."

So we did. Dad leaned against the deck rail, and Homer and I got in the big canvas hammock. We lay across it sideways so our feet touched the deck, and swung back and forth.

Joy stretched out by Dad. Looking up at the stars, we sang, "The Eyes of Texas Are Upon You."

Afterwards, Homer said, "You know, when I was little, and we'd just moved here from Georgia, I'd hear that song and be scared to death."

I burst out laughing.

"Well, you know," he explained, sort of embarrassed, "it says 'the eyes of Texas are upon you, you cannot get away.' I used to look around and wonder where the eyes were, and when they'd get me."

Dad let out a whoop, and I almost fell out of the hammock I was laughing so hard.

Homer started laughing, too, and then we couldn't stop. After a while Dad started playing "Buffalo Gal Wont'cha Come Out Tonight?" but we'd totally lost it, so he gave up and went in the house.

Homer and I stayed there, winding down and swinging back and forth. Finally I said, "Anything special you want to do before you leave?"

"Yeah. I want to get an 'A' in math, so Dad'll be proud of me."

"I can help you," I offered. (Picture halo over my head.)

Homer looked at me. "You get good grades in math? I don't need any C+ coaching."

I jumped up, ready to dump him out of the hammock, but he was grinning. I dumped him out, anyway.

~ ~ ~

Since Howie wouldn't be returning to our house, I moved back into my own room with Homer, and you know what? It was kinda fun having a roommate. Joy slept with me, mostly, but sometimes with Homer, too. Homer and I spent the afternoons working on math—he just needed some extra explaining, playing basketball and goofing off in the tree house with Andi. At night we lay there in the dark talking about all kinds of stuff.

One night Homer said, "You know, even though Howie and I are twins, I'm the youngest, and he never lets me forget it."

"What do you mean, the youngest?" I asked.

"He was born two minutes before me."

I laughed. "So you were even a slow-poke getting born."

Homer snorted. "I think he elbowed me out of the way."

"Well, maybe in Colorado, you can be in different classes."

"Yeah."

"I sure wish I hadn't called him names," I said. "I feel real guilty about it."

"Aw, he had it coming."

I was surprised he said that. Sometimes Homer had been pretty mean, himself. But since he did, I said, "He just made me so mad, picking on Andi. And picking on me. Why is he like that, I wonder?"

Homer didn't answer at first. Then he said, "I don't know. I think he's a lot like Dad. Dad says things, too, sometimes. Just blows up. Mostly at Howie when he talks back to him. They both have pretty bad tempers. I feel guilty sometimes too, because it's…" He was quiet a second. "…easier not having him around. But," he added real quick, "I'll be glad when he comes home."

"Right," I said. I knew I'd sure felt that way, but I hadn't thought Homer did. Wow.

Another night we had the radio tuned to our favorite station, and Homer said, "You think your dad would show me some chords on the guitar?"

"Sure. But I hope you're not planning on singing."

Homer *zinged* me with a pillow, right in the face, and you know what that started. We turned on the light and were jumping from one bed to another, whacking each other with pillows, when Dad opened the door.

He smiled and quoted lines from one of his favorite movies, "Cider House Rules", where Michael Caine checks on the boys in the orphanage before they go to sleep: "Good night, you princes of Maine, you kings of New England." Then he turned off the light.

I had to explain it.

"I like the way he talks," Homer said.

~ ~ ~

Dad had a ball teaching Homer chords. Homer was a pretty fast learner, and he had a ball, too, accompanying himself while he sang off key. I guess it's easier to learn something you really want to learn, especially if you want to learn it in a hurry. Before long, school would be out and he'd be leaving.

I used to count the days and weeks until they'd be gone and I could have my own room back. Heck, my own life back. But now that it was almost time, I didn't really want Homer to leave. 'Course I'd never tell him that.

Homer spent the weekend with his mother and visited Howie a lot. When he came back Sunday night he was real depressed. I guess Mom knew he would be because she had his favorite spaghetti and meatballs for supper. But he didn't eat much.

Later, when we were in our beds, I heard him crying. I didn't want to embarrass him, but I couldn't just ignore it. So I said what my psychologist mom always says, "You want to talk about it?"

He didn't, at first. I must have been just about asleep when he said, "It's gonna take a long time for Howie to get well. He's real thin, and he's having a hard time in physical therapy trying to learn to walk again."

He hadn't told me that before. I guess it hadn't dawned on me that whatever was wrong in his brain could keep him from walking. I didn't know what to say at first, but then I did. "Will he be able to move to Colorado?"

"Not anytime soon."

And it just slipped out. "You mean you can stay?"

Homer turned on the light. "You want me to?"

I grinned. "Yeah, I do."

CHAPTER EIGHTEEN

GRANDPA IN TROUBLE

The police said they found Grandpa "wandering" around the neighborhood in his pajamas. They tried to take him home, but he got mad and told them he hadn't finished his walk, so they took him down to the station and called us.

I listened to Mom and Dad talking. The words, "Alzheimer's Disease" came up. Mom sounded like she was going to cry. She called the Dalrymples to see if Joy and I could stay with them for a little while, and then they left. It was a Friday and Homer was with his mom.

Andi and I looked up Alzheimer's on Google. It is one scary disease, let me tell you. And the worse thing is there's no cure.

I hadn't noticed anything different lately about Grandpa. He seemed normal and happy to me. He just forgot stuff sometimes. But, so did Mom. Heck, so did I.

Except there was this one time a few weeks ago. It was the weekend and I was spending the night with him and we decided to take a walk. It was about nine o'clock. We were going along, enjoying being outside, and we saw this lady waving at her window. Grandpa thought she was waving at him, so he went over where he could see her better and waved back. She screamed, and we took off. Turned out she called the police. While we were finishing our walk they pulled up and stopped us.

The old lady's story was she was dancing! Can you believe it? She sure must've been waving her arms around a lot. While I was trying to explain what happened, Grandpa was muttering, "How was I supposed to know she was dancing? I thought she was waving. The old bat should've been *glad* somebody waved at her." The policeman shook his head and suggested we get on home.

Mom must've heard about it, though we sure hadn't told her.

~ ~ ~

Dad came for me at the Dalrymple's when they got back from the police station. They'd brought Grandpa home with them, and Dad said he was spittin' nails he was so mad.

"I was taking a walk! I was not wandering!" Grandpa sputtered. "Minding my own business, too, not bothering anybody…. not *waving* at anybody."

Mom looked worried and upset. "But Dad, you were… are… in your pajamas."

"So what? I'm covered up. These are my best 'going-out-of-town' pajamas. Fancy ones! Those cops should be glad I wasn't in my underwear."

That was a visual I could do without. Pretty funny, though. It's a good thing I was out of the guest room, because that's where Mom put Grandpa. She gave him some warm milk to help him sleep.

When I went in to tell him goodnight he'd calmed down. He took off his glasses and rubbed his eyes. "Travis, gettin' old is not for sissies. You do perfectly normal things and people think you're off your rocker."

"Um, I don't think walking around the neighborhood in your pajamas is exactly normal, Grandpa, but I don't think you're off your rocker."

"Well, that's good."

"But, hey! How 'bout if I go with you next time? I'll wear my pajamas, too. It'll be an adventure."

He chuckled and gave me a hug. I could hear him laughing off and on when I went to bed. But I couldn't sleep. I kept thinking about what Andi and I had read on the Internet. What if Grandpa had gotten lost? What if he forgot where he lived? How scary was that?

Sometimes when I remind Grandpa of something he forgot, he says I'm a good reminderer, and that it's a good thing for a grandson to be. Well, if that's what my grandpa needs, I'll be the best dang reminderer he ever saw.

It was a long night. It was a good thing the next day was Saturday. When Joy and I went to check on Grandpa in the morning he was gone. Mom said he'd left early. We went over to his house.

"Why'd you leave, Grandpa?"

"Wanted to get home. Travis, there's not a darn thing wrong with me except old age. I don't have Alzheimer's, and I don't have dementia. I'm just a mite forgetful, and I do what I feel like doing. Folks ought to be able to do that when they get old—as long as they don't hurt anybody."

"Grandpa, is there some medicine that would help you remember things better?"

"I reckon there is. They got medicine for just about everything, now. Even limp noodles. Know what I'm… ?"

"Got it, Grandpa."

"Good. There might come a time when…"

"Grandpa! Um… maybe you better get some memory medicine. And I'll help you remember to take it."

"You will? Well, come to think of it, I think there's some called chocolate fudge ice cream. Maybe we can take it together."

I don't think there's a thing wrong with my grandpa, except he says embarrassing things, sometimes. But that night I had nightmares about Howie.

CHAPTER NINETEEN

ANDI'S IDEA and HOMER'S GOOF

I couldn't get Howie out of my mind—that he had to learn to walk again. I tried to think what it would be like. I'd been having nightmares about him falling and he couldn't get up, like that commercial for old people.

Up in the tree house we talked about it.

"He holds himself up between these two bars," Homer said, "and tries to walk. It's real hard, he says. And even though his arm is mostly mended, it still hurts some. It's helping to build up the strength in his arms, though."

"I wish there was something we could do for him," I said.

Andi clapped her hands. "*I* know. Let's make him some cupcakes. And Homer, you can take them when you go see him tomorrow. Maybe they'll help him put on some weight."

I'd never made cupcakes before, but live and learn, as Mom says. We climbed down and went to find Andi's mother. She was up in her studio, drawing.

"Mom, we want to make some cupcakes for Howie," Andi said. "Do we have the stuff, or can we go get it?"

"Well, let's take a look," said Mrs. D.

Down in their kitchen, she checked the ingredients. "We've got flour, sugar, baking powder, milk, eggs, oil and vanilla," she said.

"And cocoa and powdered sugar to make the icing," added Andi. That's everything."

Her mom got out the bowl, hand mixer and cupcake tins. She turned on the oven.

"Have fun," she said.

Naturally Andi had made them before, so she knew how much stuff to put in. We got the batter ready and poured it into those little paper things that go in the tins and put them in the oven. Then we started on the icing. Andi was using the electric hand mixer and Homer said he wanted to do it, so she let him. Homer beat for awhile, then he said, "I think that's enough," and lifted the beaters out of the bowl.

Chocolate icing flew everywhere! In our faces, all over the stove, cabinets, counter, walls, ceiling. And Joy.

"Turn it off! Turn it off!" Andi yelled.

What a mess! We looked around, horrified. It was so awful we started laughing. Everybody looked so funny. Joy looked like a Dalmation! We *all* looked like Dalmations! I wish I'd had my camera.

"Man, that thing is powerful!" Homer said, licking icing off his arm.

Still giggling, Andi wet some sponges and got a mop and we went to work cleaning up.

We took turns using the sponge mop on the ceiling and the high part of the cabinets. Joy helped with the floor, licking up icing but we finally had to take her outside and hose her off. The whole thing took a long time. Every now and then somebody would bust out laughing and that would set us off again.

"What's going on down there?" Mrs. D. called from upstairs.

"Nothing," we all yelled at the same time.

It's a good thing she was busy and didn't come check. We did our best to get it all, but I bet she'll be finding chocolate icing in weird places for months.

We finally got the kitchen cleaned up and the cupcakes iced. Time to eat, and boy were they good. Too bad there wasn't a video of Homer and the icing, though. That was truly awesome!

I hoped they would make Howie feel better. But to tell you the truth, I don't think food, no matter how good it was, would make me feel better if I couldn't walk.

CHAPTER TWENTY

HOPE

Monday was the first day of the last week of school, and that afternoon Andi, Homer and I were back in the tree house. We'd given up on the spy idea. It was a good safe house though. A fun, safe place to be.

"Howie said the cupcakes were great, and thank you," Homer said. "He even laughed at the flying icing story."

I snickered, thinking about it. "How's he doing with the walking?"

"He's getting a little better," Homer said. "And he's talking pretty good."

"That's great."

Later, Homer and I had hardly gotten home when Andi called. "Guys, see if you can come over for supper and a movie tonight. There's this really neat one I want you to see, and Mom says it's okay. Travis, tell your mother we'll eat early so you won't get home too late."

There wasn't much going on at school, so she let us go. Andi opened the door. "I've been wanting you guys to see this. I love it and I think you'll like it, too. And after supper I'll make us ice cream sundaes!"

Homer grinned. "It must be a chic flick if you have to bribe us."

Actually it was a musical called Camelot. And we did love it. It was about King Arthur and the knights of the Round Table. Andi's favorite part was Sir Lancelot singing "C'est Moi" (pronounced 'say mwah,' which means 'it is I')—bragging about what a great knight he was. The words were hilarious. Also it had knights jousting with long, pointed lances. Man, those things were powerful. And old Merlin had these eyes that glowed. But at the end I really felt sorry for King Arthur. Between Lancelot and Mordred ruining everything and destroying the Round Table, and Guinevere leaving him, he got dumped on, big time.

That night, in bed, I thought about how things can happen to you that you'd never think would happen, like what happened to Howie and King Arthur. And there's a lot of stuff we do, without paying any attention to it, like walking. It's got to take a lot of guts to learn how all over again. Sorta like King Arthur going on with his life without his wife, his best friend, and his dream. It sure makes the past five months of my life seem like a piece of cake in comparison.

~ ~ ~

During our last week of school I kept trying to picture Howie doing what I was doing, as I went up and down stairs a million times lugging my backpack, and running around outside. I wondered when he'd be able to run. I had an idea.

When Friday finally came, the kids in our class told Homer to have fun in Colorado, and sent best wishes to Howie. Homer had made some new friends the past few weeks. Mrs. Parks piled a stack of catch-up work for Howie on Homer and me, so he wouldn't be so far behind in the fall.

And guess what? Homer got an A in math! (Halo's glowin'.)

We were free!

~ ~ ~

That weekend Andi painted the wall in my room at Grandpa's. She put in a field with cattle grazing and a tank (which is a man-made pond) and a windmill. A big oak tree in one corner had branches that spread way out on both walls. And best of all, she painted me throwing a tennis ball for Joy, and Grandpa sitting on the fence, watching. We loved it! That girl has awesome talent!

Sunday afternoon, Andi filled a Styrofoam cooler with cold lemonade, cookies and paper cups and pulled it up into the tree house with the pulley. My old backpack hung from a limb with some binoculars, a legal pad and pens, and a bag of peanuts-in-the-shell in it. Homer nailed a TV dinner tray onto a limb, to hold the peanuts for the squirrels.

There was this one squirrel that was braver than the others. If you sat real still, he'd run down the limb and grab a peanut right out of your hand. He even got kind of cocky and dropped shells on us from branches above. We decided to name him Sir Lancelot. Lance, for short.

One day, about two weeks after school was out, the three of us were shooting baskets when Aunt Karen pulled her car into our driveway. The passenger door opened and we could see Howie's head. As we watched, he slowly pulled himself out. He wobbled, and I held my breath. Then he turned, and just stood there. I looked through the windshield at Aunt Karen. She had one hand over her mouth, but I guess she knew he had to do this by himself.

Homer ran over and grabbed him in a big bear hug, almost knocking him down. Then Andi hugged him, too. I stood there, thinking I didn't know if I wanted to actually hug him. So I went over and said, Welcome home!"

Boy, did he look different. Besides being thinner, he looked older. But the main thing I noticed was he didn't look angry any more.

Okay, you guys," he said. "Stand back and watch a first class 'power-walk'."

We all moved back some. Howie let go of the car door, held his arms out a little from his sides and shuffled slowly toward us. I don't know about the others, but I was holding my breath again. He was really concentrating, one step at a time. He'd move one foot forward, take a breath, and move the other one. Then he'd rest a second, and start again. When he got closer to us, he grinned. I glanced at Andi. She had tears in her eyes. So did Homer. Heck, I guess I did, too.

Suddenly I felt Dad's hands on my shoulders. I leaned back against him, and he crossed his arms over my chest. It made me feel like everything was going to be all right.

He and Mom must have been on the front porch, watching. They probably knew Howie and Aunt Karen were coming. Boy, I sure didn't. What a surprise!

We all clapped and cheered. Then we went inside. Andi ran to get her mom and Charlie.

It turned out the plan was for Howie to spend the night with us while his mom finished packing. Then she and Uncle Henry would come get them in the morning and head for Colorado. Man, when things started happening, they happened fast.

After Andi and Charlie and their mom left, Homer and I took Howie for a walk up the sidewalk to the corner and back, one of us on each side of him. It was slow going, but he didn't seem embarrassed at all to hold on to us. He leaned from side to side, walking kind of bumpy.

When we turned around to come back, I finally got up the courage to say what had been on my mind ever since he got hurt. "Howie, I'm sorry I called you names. I've been feeling real bad about it."

He stopped. "Good. I've been feeling bad about you, too, picking on you and stuff, so we're even. High five."

Homer let go of Howie so he could reach up to slap my hand, but Howie lost his balance and almost fell. I grabbed both his arms. We were tilting, face to face.

"Want to dance?" I said.

He slowly straightened up, shaking his head. Then he laughed. "I didn't feel *that* bad about you."

I laughed, too, and Homer got his other arm again.

Howie looked over at the tree house. "Next time I'm here I'm gonna climb that thing."

"Yeah, you'll have to meet Lance, our squirrel friend," Homer said. "He'll eat out of your hand."

Howie looked around at the sky and the trees and everything. He took a deep breath. "Man, you don't know how good it feels just to be outside. I thought I'd never get out of that hospital."

"You're going to a great place to be outside," I said, "the mountains and all that snow. You'll have to send pictures. And build a snowman for me."

Homer looked around Howie at me. "Shoot, you'll have to come see us."

I grinned. "That'd be awesome."

"Dad says he's going to get me some snow shoes," Howie said, "since I probably won't be able to ski for awhile. I was really looking forward to learning, too."

"Yeah, but you can clomp around like Big Foot," I said. "Much more intense."

Howie snorted.

"And I bet it won't be long before you *can* ski," I added. "You've got all summer to build up your strength."

"Gonna do my best," he said.

That night I took my sleeping bag in with Homer and Howie so we could talk. It was good to see them happy. But they mostly talked to each other. I fell asleep.

The next morning we were all out in the driveway. Uncle Henry was putting Homer's stuff in their car while Aunt Karen talked to Mom. Andi came over to say goodbye. When she hugged Howie, he said, "Thanks for the cupcakes and the cards. I know they were your idea. These clunk-heads wouldn't have thought of it."

I'd never seen Andi blush before, but she did.

"You're welcome," she said. "Just keep getting better."

Homer punched me in the arm. "I'll text you, okay?"

"Okay," I said, punching him back.

"I won't," Howie said, grinning.

I looked at him and handed him my prized possession. "Well, maybe you can do something useful like getting the strength back in your legs with this."

He stared at me, speechless for probably the first time in his life. He looked down at Tim Duncan's autograph. "I can't take this, Roach Face," he finally said, and tried to hand it back.

I laughed. "Looks like you got the strength back in your mouth, all right."

He laughed, too, and held the basketball against his chest. "Thanks," he said.

There were more thank-yous and hugs. Then they were gone. Just like that.

Next thing I knew I was being hugged by Andi. "That was awesome!" she said in my ear.

Dad gave me a thumbs up, and Mom sent me one of her special smiles. Wow! I felt pretty good for losing my most prized possession.

Later, at lunch, with just Mom and Dad and me at the table, it felt kinda empty. But it felt good, too. What am I saying? It felt great! I was all ready to bite into my ham and cheese, when Dad cleared his throat. "Well, son, what did you glean from that experience?"

I grinned. "I 'gleaned' that five months is a heck of a long time!" I took a big bite.

Silence. The old exasperated look from parents. I put my sandwich down, chewing as fast as I could, and started over. "I learned there are reasons people act like they do. Maybe things aren't good at home. Maybe their lives suck. And I learned that name calling can come back to haunt you, big time. No more of that for me."

They looked at each other and smiled, then back at me, still expectant.

What? That wasn't enough? I tried a compliment. "You two were the best for taking them in for so long and putting up with everything from all of us."

Mom rolled her eyes.

Then I remembered what Grandpa said and how sad Howie and Homer had been. "And I think, to be a friend, you need to be understanding about stuff."

Mom reached over and squeezed my hand.

Dad nodded his head several times. "Well said! And I want you to know your mother and I think, on the whole, you did a fine job. It was tougher on you than we thought it would be. You not only had to give up your room, but you had to share your place in the family. I think we were concentrating more on helping the twins than worrying about how it would affect you. And for that, we're sorry." He took a deep breath then smiled, broadly. "But you survived! And we believe you've matured a bit. We're very proud of you!"

"Thank you, sir." I got up and grabbed Joy's leash. "Come on, girl, let's take a walk." Joy jumped all around, whapping me with her tail. I felt good. I felt great! And I just realized something. When Dad said I'd matured a bit, I guess 'a bit' was probably not as much as 'a lot', but hey, a compliment is a compliment.

I loved it.

Printed in the United States
By Bookmasters